NEWS AND THE MEDIA

by Emilie Dufresne

KNOW THE ISSUES

Enslow
PUBLISHING

Please visit our website, www.enslow.com. For a free color catalog of all our high-quality books, call toll free 1-800-398-2504 or fax 1-877-980-4454.

Cataloging-in-Publication Data
Names: Dufresne, Emilie.
Title: News and the media / Emilie Dufresne.
Description: New York : Enslow Publishing, 2021. | Series: Know the issues | Includes glossary and index.
Identifiers: ISBN 9781978516878 (pbk.) | ISBN 9781978516892 (library bound) | ISBN 9781978516885 (6 pack)
Subjects: LCSH: Media literacy--Juvenile literature. | Mass media--Juvenile literature. | Journalism--Juvenile literature.
Classification: LCC P96.M4 D847 2020 | DDC 070.4'3--dc23

Published in 2021 by
Enslow Publishing
101 West 23rd Street, Suite #240
New York, NY 10011

Front cover – Lenscap Photography, Maxx-Studio, Andrey Arkusha, Macrovector, Maglara. 2 – Macrovector, Maglara, Maxx-Studio. 3 – Andrey Arkusha, Lenscap Photography. 4 – Andrey_Popov, Maxx-Studio. 5 – qvist, Michael Dechev, Dmitri Ma, pixinoo, Bloomicon, Daniel Krason. 6 – Castleski, Hadrian, 32 pixels, Tond Van Graphcraft. 7 – Casimiro PT, MonsterDesign. 8 & 9 – chrisdorney, tanuha2001, rvlsoft, Pan Xunbin, thelefty, IB Photography, drserg, jakkapan, iPortret, Everett Collection, I. Pilon, RossEdwardCairney. 10 – Concept Photo, HQuality, Dmi T. 11 – Rawpixel.com, Stoyan Yotov, Avector, WhiteDragon. 12 – one photo, Paladin12. 13 – M-SUR, Photo Kozyr, LightField Studios. 14 – Buncha Lim, Lightspring, Bluemoon 1981, Iconic Bestiary. 15 – ashok india, michaeljung. 16 – Georgejmclittle, sirtravelalot, foxaon1987, ProStockStudio. 17 – Ollyy, 13_Phunkod. 18 – kenary820. 19 – Spectral-Design, Tero Vesalainen. 20 – Jacob Lund, guruXOX, In-Finity. 21 – wellphoto, Nejron Photo. 22 – Tawan Jz, Allen.G, emojoez. 23 – Evan Lorne, weedezign. 24 – Africa Studio, New Africa, MSSA. 25 – Jinga, Monkey Business Images. 26 – Rawpixel.com. 27 – Tinseltown, Alena Ozerova. 28 – Multiverse, M.M.art. 29 – PedroNevesDesign. Sam Aronov. 30 – Chatcharin Sombutpinyo, 2p2play. Post It Notes throughout – rzarek, Lyudmyla Kharlamova. Images are courtesy of Shutterstock.com. With thanks to Getty Images, Thinkstock Photo and iStockphoto.

Manufactured in the United States of America

CPSIA compliance information: Batch #BS20ENS: For further information contact Enslow Publishing, New York, New York, at 1-800-398-2504.

CONTENTS

Words that look like **THIS** are explained in the glossary on page 31.

WHAT IS THE NEWS?

NEWS

When we say "the news," we are talking about new information and recent events that have happened in the world. This is then shown to us through different types of media. Some news is local, and tells us about events that are happening in our county or nation.

We can get news from TV broadcasts, online articles, and newspapers.

NEWS

NEWS
Monday, April 1, 2015
Final Edition
Your Information Source
167/21

Internet Is Sweeping The World Faster Than Electricity!!!

We are all part of a **GLOBAL COMMUNITY**, so it is important to know what is happening in the world.

Some news is international; it tells us about events all over the world. Nowadays, travel around the world is quicker and we are all **CONNECTED** by the internet. This means that we can receive news from around the world almost as soon as it happens.

WHAT IS THE MEDIA?

MEDIA

When we say the media, we are talking about different types of MASS COMMUNICATION. Media allows us to communicate with people all over the world.

TRADITIONAL

There are two types of media, traditional and social.

SOCIAL

Newspapers, magazines, radio, and TV are all types of traditional media. This type of media provides entertainment and information about current events. Social media refers to websites and applications we use to follow celebrities and communicate with our friends and families. Social media is more interactive and allows us to share our creativity.

NEWS AND THE MEDIA

The news is what is said and the media is the way the news is shown to us. If we are reading a newspaper article, the newspaper is the type of media, and the content of the article is the news.

One news story could be told in lots of different ways through different types of media.

BREAKING NEWS
FIREFIGHTER RISKS LIFE SAVING KITTEN

BREAKING NEWS
KITTEN RESCUED AFTER GETTING STUCK IN TREE

BREAKING NEWS
NEAR DEATH; A KITTEN'S TALE

LIVE

BREAKING NEWS

These headlines are all reporting the same story.

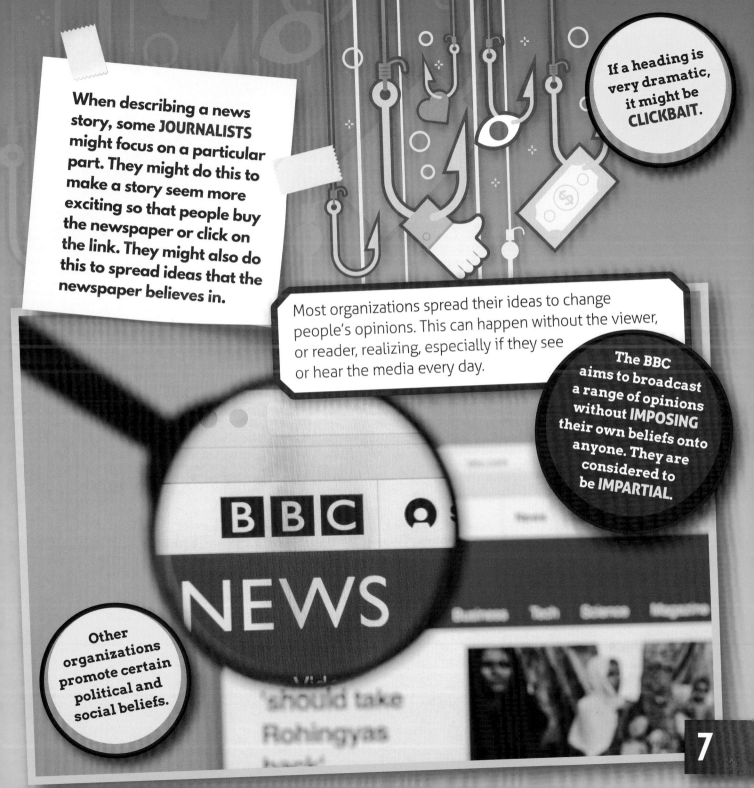

When describing a news story, some **JOURNALISTS** might focus on a particular part. They might do this to make a story seem more exciting so that people buy the newspaper or click on the link. They might also do this to spread ideas that the newspaper believes in.

If a heading is very dramatic, it might be **CLICKBAIT**.

Most organizations spread their ideas to change people's opinions. This can happen without the viewer, or reader, realizing, especially if they see or hear the media every day.

The BBC aims to broadcast a range of opinions without **IMPOSING** their own beliefs onto anyone. They are considered to be **IMPARTIAL**.

Other organizations promote certain political and social beliefs.

BBC NEWS

who should take Rohingyas back?

MEDIA THROUGHOUT HISTORY

15TH CENTURY
Johannes Gutenberg invents the printing press, allowing books to be MASS PRODUCED. They no longer had to be handwritten and more and more people had access to books.

17TH CENTURY
Newspapers are circulated in many European countries, including Germany, the Netherlands, France, Portugal, and England.

1895
The world's first commercial movie screening takes place at the Grand Café in Paris.

2010
Kevin Systrom and Mike Krieger create the social media platform Instagram in San Francisco, California. Facebook bought Instagram for about $1 billion in 2012.

2006
Twitter is launched.

2005
The video-sharing site YouTube is launched.

1906

On December 24, 1906, the first entertainment and music radio broadcast is transmitted from Brant Rock, Massachusetts, to the public.

1950s

By the 1950s, many households and businesses had a television set.

1990

Sir Tim Berners-Lee invents the World Wide Web, which allows people to share information all over the world.

2004

Facebook, a social networking site, is launched.

2003

Social networking sites take off. Myspace, one of the biggest social networks at the time, is launched.

1999

One of the first popular instant-messaging sites, Windows Live Messenger (MSN), is launched.

MEDIA TOMORROW

Although media has come a long way, it is still growing and changing along with new TECHNOLOGIES. There are lots of new types of media that we will be seeing more frequently in the next few years.

WHAT TOMORROW'S MEDIA MIGHT LOOK LIKE

Addressable TV is a form of advertising where the commercials you see are chosen based on your likes, interests, and location. Instead of scheduled television shows having set commercials, each home will see different commercials based on their interests.

Augmented Reality (AR) is a type of technology that mixes computer-generated images with the world around us. It is mostly used in games. Developers want to make augmented reality more MAINSTREAM. It could aid in the delivery of news stories on both traditional and social media, and modernize advertising.

AR games like *Pokemon Go* are only the beginning.

Live streaming has become more and more popular in the last year, with celebrities using it to talk directly to fans. Social media and news companies are looking to use more live-streaming features. Live streaming will allow the latest news events to reach audiences very quickly.

MEDIA AND CENSORSHIP

WHAT IS CENSORSHIP?

Censorship is when a government or organization **PROHIBITS** certain information from being published in the media.

Some censorship is needed. For example, age restrictions are seen as a good thing because they stop young children from seeing things that might upset them.

████████████, during ████████ World War I, ████████ lots of letters████ looked like this. ████████ certain things ████████ were blacked-out so that ██ the important secrets would not ████████ go to the enemy.

Nowadays, some people's beliefs are censored in the media in order to influence the public's opinions. In some countries there is more censorship than in others.

Countries like the U.S. and Canada have a free press. This means that people are free to publish any opinion they want and are free to criticize the government.

CENSORSHIP

FREEDOM OF SPEECH

Scandinavian countries, like Sweden and Finland, have the least RESTRICTED press. Countries such as North Korea and Syria have the most restricted press.

NEWS AND BIAS

Sometimes it is hard to tell what is fact and what is opinion.

A fact is something that has been proven to be true. An opinion is a belief that is not necessarily based on fact or knowledge.

Bias is when a particular opinion is shown instead of telling the facts.

A reporter is biased if:
- They give their opinions about an event.
- They give more attention to events that support their opinion.
- They only tell one side of the story.

Both online and traditional news articles can be biased. It is important to be able to spot bias in the news because the way the news is told can change our views of news events.

14

Sometimes it is okay for journalists and reporters to show their bias, as long as the viewer or reader is aware that it is an opinion and not a fact. The reader or viewer can then decide for themselves if they agree with them or not.

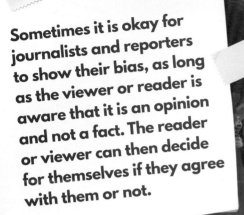

Sometimes spotting bias is easy. Journalists or reporters might say things like "I think..." or "I believe...", which lets you know they are giving an opinion. Sometimes spotting bias is hard. If you can't tell if it is an opinion or fact, ask yourself some questions about the article.

SPOTTING BIAS

WHO IS SPEAKING?

DOES THE ARTICLE SHOW ANYONE IN A VERY BAD OR VERY GOOD WAY?

ARE THEY DISCUSSING ONE VIEWPOINT MORE THAN ANOTHER?

ARE THE WORDS IN THE TITLE VERY DRAMATIC?

FAKE NEWS

Just as some news sources may be biased, some may be made up or EXAGGERATED. This type of news is called fake news. It is very easy for people to post online, which means they can write whatever they want and make it look like a real news article.

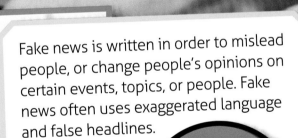

Fake news is written in order to mislead people, or change people's opinions on certain events, topics, or people. Fake news often uses exaggerated language and false headlines.

If a news article has a title that is too good to be true, it probably is.

It can be easy to trust fake news articles. This is because they can be published on sites that we trust, such as Facebook, Google, and Twitter. However, these websites and social media platforms do not know who has written these articles.

Most articles we see are chosen by **ALGORITHMS** rather than real people. Algorithms do not check to see if an article is real or not.

If someone we trust has shared an article, we might assume that the article can be trusted. We must always question whether an article is trying to change our opinion or not.

STAYING SAFE ONLINE

THINGS TO REMEMBER

There are a few things to remember that will help you stay safe online.

- Never give out your personal information, such as your address or phone number.
- Don't give your passwords to anyone.
- Remember that not everyone online is who they say they are.
- Remember that once you've put a picture or video of yourself online, a lot of people can see it and download it.
- Don't meet up with anyone you've met online unless a parent or guardian is with you.
- Always make sure an adult knows what you are doing online.

ALWAYS ASK

If anything online confuses you, or you are not sure it is appropriate for your age group, always ask an adult.

BEING RESPECTFUL ONLINE

You're ugly

Lots of people go online and post nasty comments on people's pictures, statuses, and videos, just to hurt their feelings. Often, they do this just to get a reaction out of someone. If someone makes a comment you think is mean, tell an adult.

Never be horrible to other people online. If they are mean to you, you shouldn't be mean back.

JOBS IN THE MEDIA

CONTENT CREATOR:
Content creators can be writers, designers, and video makers, among other things. They are often creative people who use media as a way to express that creativity. They could work for a company or create content for themselves.

CAMERA OPERATOR: Camera operators record all sorts of things for films and TV shows. They work with the director to get the right visual style. This job uses a lot of technology.

Because there are many different types of media, there are lots of different jobs you can have.

JOURNALIST:

Journalists gather information on different events. They then report this news on TV or in newspapers, articles, or documentaries. Some journalists specialize in certain events. For example, a sports journalist will cover sporting events, whereas a foreign correspondent will report on events happening across the world.

SOUND ENGINEER: Sound engineers can work in recording studios, theater, radio stations, or game companies. There are lots of different types of sound engineers. Some types record sound files in studios, some balance the volumes for live events, and some make sure all the sound equipment is working.

ADVERTISING

WHAT IS AN AD?

YOUR AD HERE

An advertisement, or ad, is something that is shown to the public to sell a product or service. Lots of companies and organizations make ads and show them on both traditional and social media. These companies pay to have their ads in certain places, such as the first page of the newspaper or at the top of a news feed of a social media platform.

Ads can get annoying when they are playing in the middle of a video you are watching. However, ads are important because they fund the things we like. Companies pay TV channels and other media platforms to run their ads. This money then goes towards making more shows we like.

We see hundreds of ads every day. There are so many ads we might not notice when we see one.

WHAT IS AND ISN'T AN AD?

Google

It is important to know what is and isn't an ad. It is easier to spot an ad in traditional media. It is harder to tell online and on social media.

Google Search   I'm Feeling

When we look up something on a search engine such as Google, the first few results that we see are usually sponsored. This means that a company has paid for their website link to appear first.

Video Advertising

Sometimes, something that doesn't look like an ad will say it is in the SMALL PRINT.

If a website, video, or post is an ad, it should tell you that it is. If you see "#ad" in the title or description of a YouTube video, it means that a company has paid for the video to be made.

THE MEDIA AND YOU

Different types of media change the way we see the world and also the way we see ourselves. Newspapers, magazines, and online media all edit photos of celebrities. Photos are edited to make people look slimmer, or have flawless skin and hair.

It is important to remember that the way celebrities look in the media is not how they normally look.

It is easy to compare ourselves to these images and this can have a bad effect on our **BODY IMAGE**. It might make us think that we have to look the way the models do in the magazines.

The media should represent all different body types, and how people look in real life.

Sometimes what we see in social media can also affect how we feel about the way we live our lives. If we follow someone's Instagram or YouTube channel, we might think they have an amazing life, where they get to do lots of great things all the time. This can make us feel sad if we don't have a life like that.

It is important to remember that what people post online does not necessarily show their whole life, but just parts of their day.

Apps such as Snapchat and Instagram also have filter options, which can make things look or seem better than they are in real life.

25

DIVERSITY IN THE MEDIA

Lots of us live in communities with different types of people, who have different ages, genders, body types, and ETHNICITIES. When a community is made up of lots of different cultures and ethnicities, it is called a multicultural society.

This diversity should be represented in the media. Unfortunately, most of the time, it isn't.

Often the media focuses on white, able-bodied people. Other ethnicities and body types are shown much less in the media. It is important to see all different types of people in the media so that everyone feels included.

Many films have been criticized for not having enough racial diversity. For a long time, white actors, directors, and producers have earned the most money and won the most awards. However, recently more people of other ethnicities have been winning important awards and playing leading roles.

At the 2017 Oscars, it was the first year that every acting category had a black nominee.

Many newspapers and magazines only show very slim women. This does not reflect the diversity of different body types. In the past few years, more and more plus-sized women have been shown in the media.

Seeing people who look like us in the media can help us feel more confident in who we are.

CHANGE AND THE MEDIA

One of the great things about the media today is its ability to bring about change. Because news travels around the world so quickly today, we hear about wars, natural disasters, and HUMANITARIAN CRISES very quickly. This means that people can try to help those in need.

Hurricane Irma destroyed many Caribbean Islands and parts of the United States, and left many people either dead, homeless, or without electricity. Many humanitarian charities and funding pages raised money by using the media.

Social media also helped people work together, and helped trapped people share their location.

Sometimes online campaigns for charities might go **VIRAL**. This has happened with campaigns such as Movember, which promotes men's health. During November, people grow their facial hair to raise money and awareness for the charity.

M**O**VEMBER

Prostate Cancer Awareness Month

From 2015 to 2018, Red Nose Day raised $100 million and has helped 8 million children!

Red Nose Day is a fundraising campaign led by the organization Comic Relief Fund. Through the campaign, U.S. Walgreens stores sell red noses to raise money to help children in need have access to education, medicine to stay healthy, mental health resources, and ways to stay safe. The charity holds both TV and public fundraisers and raises millions of dollars each year.

ACTIVITY

Would you like to be a journalist? Try to conduct an interview with one of your friends. Ask them questions about themselves and write down notes.

"What is your favorite food?"

"What did you do last weekend?"

"How old are you?"

Try to write a news report about something that is happening in your school. It could be a play or a sports tournament. Think about the things you will need to say, such as the date and time, location, what happened, and who was involved.

Think about different ads you see. Come up with a catchy **SLOGAN** for a product you like and think about a new way to advertise it.

GLOSSARY

ALGORITHM	a set of rules or calculations that something or someone must follow to solve a problem
BODY IMAGE	how someone feels about the way they look
CLICKBAIT	internet content that tries to get people's attention and make them click its link
CONNECTED	joined or linked together
ETHNICITIES	groups of people that share a national or cultural tradition
EXAGGERATED	to show something as bigger, better, or worse than it is
GLOBAL COMMUNITY	all the people around the world who are connected together in different ways
HUMANITARIAN CRISES	events that could cause damage to the health, safety, and well-being of a large group of people
IMPARTIAL	treating all things equally without bias
IMPOSING	forcing a belief onto someone
JOURNALISTS	people who report the news for a newspaper, magazine, or TV channel
MAINSTREAM	describing ideas and activities that people see as normal
MASS COMMUNICATION	exchanging information on a large scale
MASS PRODUCED	to make something in large quantities through a mechanical process
PROHIBIT	to stop something from happening
RESTRICTED	when something is kept within certain limits
SLOGAN	a short and memorable phrase
SMALL PRINT	details that a company or organization doesn't want to promote and writes in a small font
TECHNOLOGIES	machines or devices that are made using scientific knowledge
VIRAL	describing something on the internet that is quickly passed between a lot of people

INDEX